BECAUSE YOU ARE MY BABY

by Sherry North illustrated by Marcellus Hall

Abrams Books for Young Readers, New York

The illustrations in this book
were created using watercolors on paper.

Library of Congress Cataloging-in-Publication Data:
North, Sherry.
Because you are my baby / by Sherry North ;
illustrated by Marcellus Hall.
p. cm.
Summary: Lists wonderful ways a parent, whether a rock star
or a geologist, could demonstrate love for a child.
ISBN-13: 978-0-8109-9482-9 (hardcover w/jkt.)
[1. Parent and child—Fiction. 2. Babies—Fiction.] I. Hall,
Marcellus, ill. II. Title.
PZ7.N8158Bec 2008
[E]—dc22
2007012758

Text copyright © 2008 Sherry North
Illustrations copyright © 2008 Marcellus Hall

Book design by Chad W. Beckerman

Published in 2008 by Abrams Books for Young Readers,
an imprint of Harry N. Abrams, Inc.

Printed and bound in China
10 9 8 7 6 5 4 3 2 1

HNA
harry n. abrams, inc.
a subsidiary of La Martinière Groupe
115 West 18th Street
New York, NY 10011
www.hnabooks.com

For Julian
—S. N.

For Nicole
—M. H.

If I were a sailor, I would sail the world with you,

With sails of cotton candy and a handy penguin crew.

If I were a mountaineer, I would take you to the peak

Of Everest and Fuji, a new summit every week.

If I were a builder, I would build a castle tall

And fill the moat with jelly beans . . .

So you could eat them all.

If I were a gardener, I would plant a trumpet vine,

With blooms that croon a jazzy tune whenever you pass by.

If I were a rock star, I would write you a hit song

And sing for you in concert from Miami to Hong Kong.

If I were a diver, we would tour the ocean floor—

Shipwrecks, crab holes, coral reefs, and much more to explore.

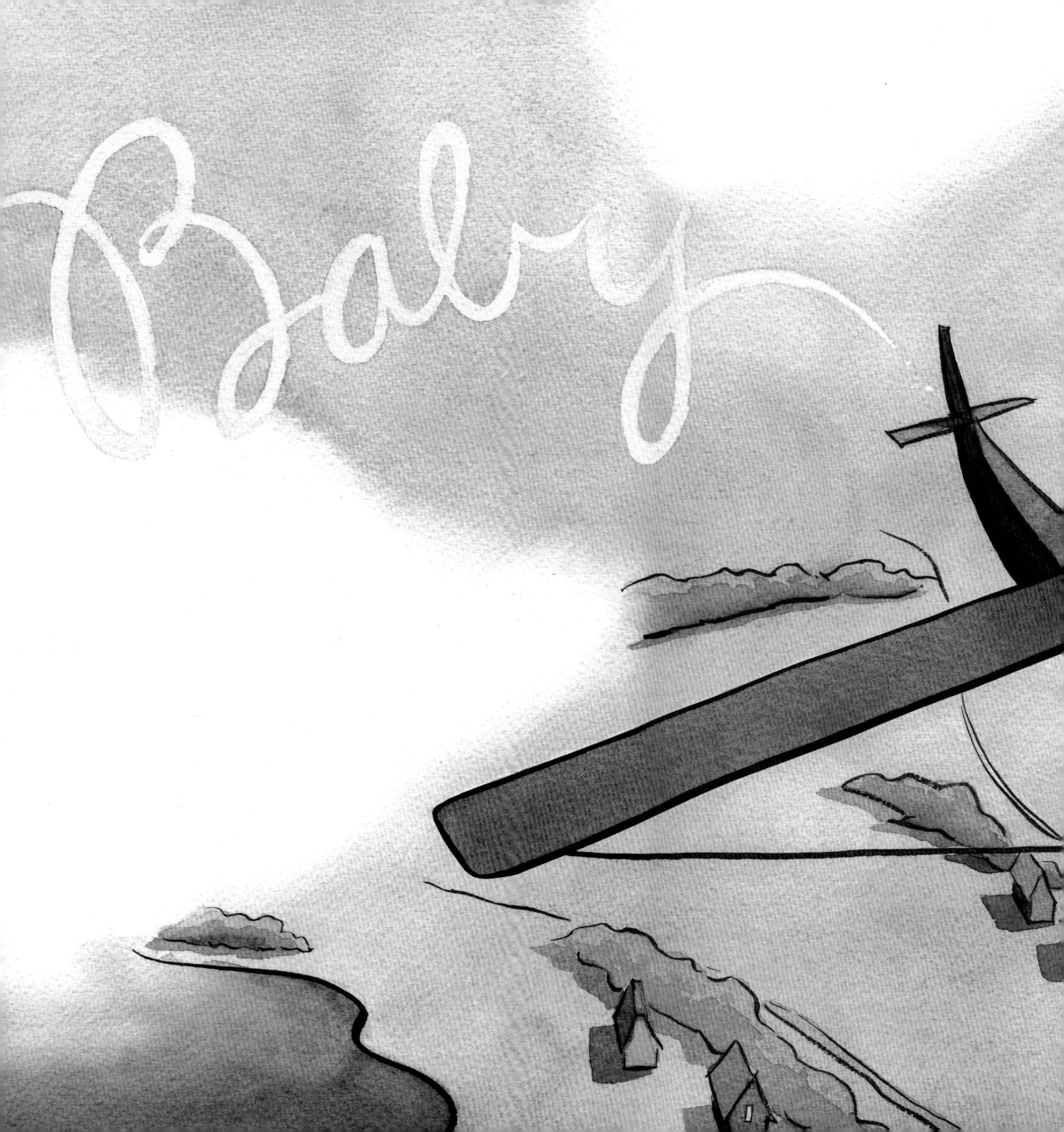
Baby

If I were a skywriter, I would write your name up high

In sparkling golden loop-the-loops across a summer sky.

If I were a geologist, I would fill your room with quartz,

Amber, turquoise, tigereye, and gemstones of all sorts.

If I were a quarterback, you would dash across the grass

And score the winning touchdown when you catch my perfect pass.

If I were an engineer, I would build a high-speed train

That lifts you off the ground and travels faster than a plane.

If I were a pizza chef, I would make a Pisa pie—

A leaning tower of mozzarella standing twelve feet high.

If I were an astronaut, we would blast off to see Mars

And cruise the red-rock surface in a pair of off-road cars.

If I were an actor, you could watch me on TV,

And I would blow a good-night kiss for only you to see.

And if I were a genie,

I would make your dreams come true . . .

Because you are my baby,

I would do anything for you.